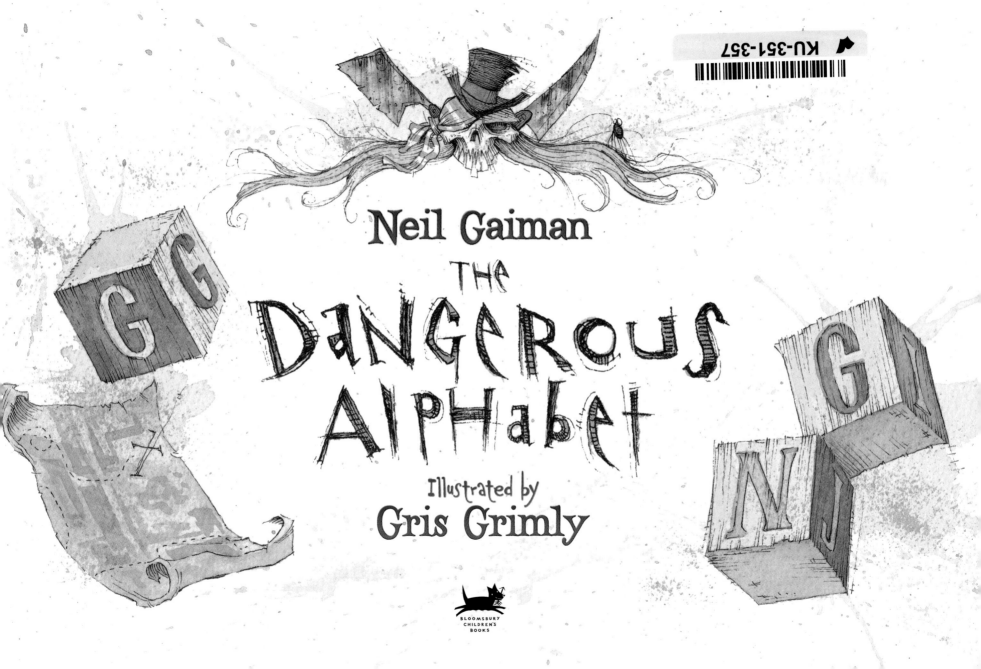

Neil Gaiman

THE Dangerous Alphabet

Illustrated by
Gris Grimly

BLOOMSBURY
CHILDREN'S
BOOKS

First published in Great Britain in 2008 by Bloomsbury Publishing Plc
36 Soho Square, London, W1D 3QY

First published in America in 2008 by HarperCollins Children's Books, a division of HarperCollins Publishers, 1350 Avenue of the Americas, New York, NY 10019
Published by arrangement with HarperCollins Children's Books, a division of HarperCollins Publishers

A CIP catalogue record of this book is available from the British Library

ISBN 978 0 7475 9711 7

Title and initials hand lettered by Gris Grimly
Design by Dana Fritts

Printed in Singapore by Tien Wah Press

1 3 5 7 9 10 8 6 4 2

All papers used by Bloomsbury Publishing Plc are natural, recyclable products
made from wood grown in well-managed forests. The manufacturing processes
conform to the environmental regulations of the country of origin.

www.bloomsbury.com

A piratical ghost story in thirteen ingenious but potentially disturbing rhyming couplets, originally conceived as a confection both to amuse and to entertain by Mr Neil Gaiman, scrivener, and then doodled, elaborated upon, illustrated, and beaten soundly by Mr Gris Grimly, etcher and illuminator, featuring two brave children, their diminutive but no less courageous gazelle, and a large number of extremely dangerous trolls, monsters, bugbears, creatures, and other such nastinesses, many of which have perfectly disgusting eating habits and ought not, under any circumstances, to be encouraged.

Please Note: The alphabet, as given in this publication, is *not to be relied upon* and has a dangerous flaw that an eagle-eyed reader may be able to discern.

A is for Always, that's where we embark.

is for Boat,

pushing off
in the dark.

D is for
DIAMONDS,
the bait on the hook.

E's for the Evil
that lures and
entices.

is for **Fear**

and its many devices.

G is for Good,
as in hero,
and Morning.

I am the author
who scratches
these rhymes.

J is the joke monsters make of their crimes.

K's but a Kiss – lovers glow with elation.

is, like 'eaven, their last destination.

M is for Mirrors you'll stare in forever.

N is for Night, and for Nothing, and Never.

is for Ovens,
far under
the street.

is for Piracy, blunt or discreet.

R is a River that flows like a dream.

S is for – somewhere – a Skull and its Smile.

T is for Treasure
heaped into a pile.

are
the reader
who
shivers
with dread.

W's **WARNINGS** went over your head.

V is for
Vile deeds
done in the
Night.

X marked the spot, if we read the map right.

(Z waits alone, and it's not for a thing.)